Dear Family and Friends of Your

Learning to read is one of the most im
your child will ever attain. Early readii
you can make it easier with Hello Readers.

Just like learning to play a sport or an instrument,
learning to read requires many opportunities to work on
skills. However, you have to get in the game or experience
real music to keep interested and motivated. Hello Readers
are carefully structured to provide the right level of text
for practice and great stories for experiencing the fun
of reading.

Try these activities:

• Reading starts with the alphabet and at the earliest level,
you may encourage your child to focus on the sounds of
letters in words and sounding out words. With more
experienced readers, focus on how words are spelled.
Be word watchers!

• Go beyond the book — talk about the story, how it
compares with other stories, and what your child likes
about it.

• Comprehension — did your child get it? Have your child
retell the story or answer questions you may ask about it.

Another thing children learn to do at this age is learn to
ride a bike. You put training wheels on to help them in the
beginning and guide the bike from behind. Hello Readers
help you support your child and then you get to watch
them take off as skilled readers.

— Francie Alexander
Chief Academic Officer
Scholastic Education

For Keith, who once swam with the dolphins.

—K.W.

To the greatest mom ever —
who has seen me through leaps big and small —
you are forever in my heart.

—D.Z.

ISBN 0-439-44159-5

Text copyright © 2003 by Kimberly Weinberger.
Illustrations copyright © 2003 by Debra Ziss.

All rights reserved. Published by Scholastic Inc.
SCHOLASTIC and associated logos are trademarks and/or registered
trademarks of Scholastic Inc.

12 11 10   8/0

Printed in the U.S.A.
First printing, April 2003

DOLPHIN'S BIG LEAP!

by Kimberly Weinberger
Illustrated by Debra Ziss

Hello Reader! — Level 1

SCHOLASTIC INC.

New York   Toronto   London   Auckland   Sydney
Mexico City   New Delhi   Hong Kong   Buenos Aires

Little Dolphin swims in the sea.

He is a part of a family.

All of the dolphins spin and slide.
They dive.
They play.
They race.
They glide.

But one thing gives
Little Dolphin a scare.
He cannot,
he will not,
jump in the air.

Each day Little Dolphin says,
"I can do it!"
Each day he says,
"There's nothing to it!"

But then he can't.
His fins won't go.
The air is too cold.
The waves are too slow.

And so one day,
Little Dolphin leaves home.
He swims through blue water.
He swims through white foam.

He swims until he sees a boat.
He sees a child
in a bright red coat.

Little Dolphin wants to play.
He forgets to be scared.
Could this be his day?

He nears the boat.
He is fast.
He is sleek.
He smiles with a mouth
that is shaped like a beak.

Then he does it.
He leaps!
He flies!

He makes a rainbow arc in the skies.

Little Dolphin whistles and clicks.
The small child claps
at her dolphin friend's tricks.

Little Dolphin waves
at the child in the coat.
He waves as he swims
away from the boat.

He swims to his family
in waters so deep.
He swims home to tell of his
    great,
      big
        LEAP!